D0468152

Electra and the Charlotte Russe

ELECTRA AND THE CHARLOTTE RUSSE

by Corinne Demas Bliss

Pictures by Michael Garland

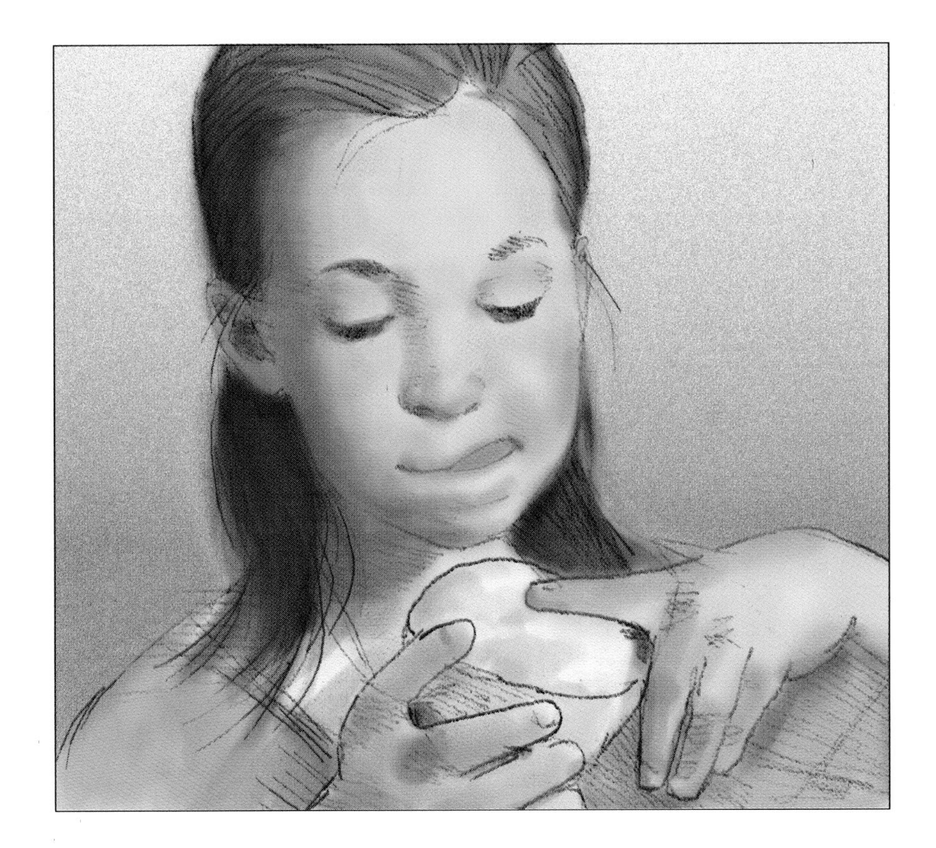

Boyds Mills Press

Published by Caroline House
Boyds Mills Press, Inc.
A Highlights Company
815 Church Street
Honesdale, Pennsylvania 18431
Printed in Mexico

Publisher Cataloging-in-Publication Data
Bliss, Corinne.
Electra and the charlotte russe / by Corinne Demas Bliss ; illustrations by Michael Garland.—1st ed.
[32]p. : col.ill. ; cm.
Summary : A misadventure ensues when a young girl goes to the bakery to buy dessert for her mother's tea party.
ISBN 1-56397-436-3
1. Greek Americans—Juvenile fiction. [1. Greek Americans—Fiction.] I. Garland, Michael, ill. II. Title.
[E]—dc20 1997 AC CIP
Library of Congress Catalog Card Number

First edition, 1997
Book designed by Tim Gillner and Michael Garland
The text of this book is set in 14-point Veljovic Medium.
The illustrations are done electronically.

10 9 8 7 6 5 4 3 2 1

In memory of Yiya
—C.D.B.

To Chelsea
—M.G.

Author's Note

When I was a little girl, my favorite stories were the ones my parents told me about their lives when they were children. Some of these stories I had them tell me again and again, and of course with each retelling the story changed and grew.

Electra and the Charlotte Russe is based on a story my mother told me about when she was a little girl. My mother's name was Electra, and she grew up in the Bronx (a part of New York City) in the early 1920s.

My daughter likes me to tell her stories about when I was a little girl, as well as the stories my mother passed on to me. Some day, I hope, she'll tell our stories along with those about her own childhood.

On Saturday Mama was having a special tea. Mrs. Papadapoulos was coming. Mrs. Marcopoulos was coming with her daughter, Athena, who was in college. And Miss Smith was coming. Miss Smith was taking Greek lessons from Mama. She was learning Greek because she was getting married to Mr. Demetropoulis and wanted to understand what his relatives said behind her back.

"Here are six nickels, Electra," said Mama. "I want you to go to the bakery and buy six charlotte russes."

Electra counted on her fingers. Mrs. Papadapoulos, Mrs. Marcopoulos, Athena, and Miss Smith. One, two, three, four. And Mama, that made five.

"The sixth one is for you," said Mama, who had eyes in the back of her head and could also read Electra's mind.

A charlotte russe is an extraordinary dessert—a circle of little cakes, called ladyfingers, topped with clouds of whipped cream. Even Mama could not make charlotte russes like the ones you could buy at the bakery. Electra tied the nickels up in her hanky and held the hanky tight in her hand. She kept her hand in her pocket, just in case.

"Remember to look up and wave to me when you get down-stairs," said Mama.

"Yes, Mama," said Electra.

"Come straight back from the bakery," said Mama, "so the cream won't spoil."

"Yes, Mama," said Electra.

"Don't lose the money," said Mama.

"Yes, Mama—I mean, no, Mama, I won't," said Electra.

Mama gave her a kiss. "*Chrisomou!*" she said, which means "my golden one." She called Electra that even though Electra's hair was dirty blond.

"*Chrisomou! Chrisomou!*" screamed Polo, the parrot, who could imitate Mama's voice so well, sometimes you couldn't tell them apart.

On the third floor landing Electra saw Murray Schwartz.

"I'm going to get a charlotte russe," she said.

"Who's that?" asked Murray.

"It's not a person, it's a dessert," said Electra. "Mama is having a party and I'm buying six of them at the bakery and one is for me to eat, myself."

"Well, goody for you," said Murray, and he stuck out his tongue.

"What happened to your tongue?" asked Electra. "It's green."

"I had a gumball," said Murray. "So there." And he stuck out his tongue again.

On the second-floor landing Mrs. DeLuca's cat was curled up on the doormat.

"I'm going to get a charlotte russe," said Electra. She was holding the money in her right hand, so she had to pat the cat with her left hand. The cat looked up at her with sleepy eyes. If he knew what a charlotte russe was, he didn't let on.

On the first floor Mr. Melnikoff was coming in after his daily walk. He was the oldest man Electra had ever known. He told her he was the oldest man in the world, but when she told Mama, Mama only laughed.

"I'm going to get a charlotte russe," she said.

"Ah," said Mr. Melnikoff. "Charlotte russe! I remember charlotte russe. A dessert fit for a princess. So you must be a princess."

"Sometimes," said Electra, and she smiled.

Outside, she almost forgot to wave up at Mama, but Mama was calling down to her. She was putting Polo out on the fire escape for his afternoon air.

“Hurry home, but don’t run,” shouted Mama.

“Don’t run,” shouted Polo. Or was it Mama? “Don’t run! Don’t run!”

Electra didn't run, but she did skip. She skipped all the way down the block and around the corner and down the next block to the bakery.

She was allowed to go to the bakery herself because she didn't have to cross any streets.

Mrs. Zimmerman, who owned the bakery, wasn't much taller than Electra and looked as if she ate nothing but pastry all day. "So what can I get for you, my dear?" she asked.

"I'd like six charlotte russes, please," said Electra. "For a party." She put the handkerchief on the counter, untied the knot, and counted out the nickels. "One, two, three, four, five—oh, no!"

"Here's 'six'!" said Mrs. Zimmerman, who spotted the last nickel caught in a fold of the handkerchief.

Mrs. Zimmerman took six charlotte russes from the glass case below the counter and laid them tenderly in a cardboard box. Each charlotte russe was in a little cardboard dish lined with a paper doily. The whipped cream was so high it came up above the sides of the box, so Mrs. Zimmerman couldn't put the box top on.

"Have a good party," said Mrs. Zimmerman, "and don't run on the way home."

Electra didn't run and she didn't skip. But she did walk very quickly because she didn't want the cream to spoil. She walked so quickly she got back to her building lickety-split. She walked so quickly she didn't see Mrs. DeLuca's cat scoot across the sidewalk. Until it was too late. Electra tripped over the cat, but she managed to hold on to the box of charlotte russes. The cat yowled and darted back to the house. Electra sat down on the front stoop to inspect the damage. Three charlotte russes were all right, but three of them had gotten mushed against the side of the box.

Electra looked up towards her apartment windows. Mama was not looking out, and Polo had been taken inside. Electra wiped the whipped cream off the side of the box, licked her fingers clean, and then carefully smoothed the cream on the three injured charlotte russes. She had to smooth away quite a lot of whipped cream to make them look right again. However, the whipped cream was delicious.

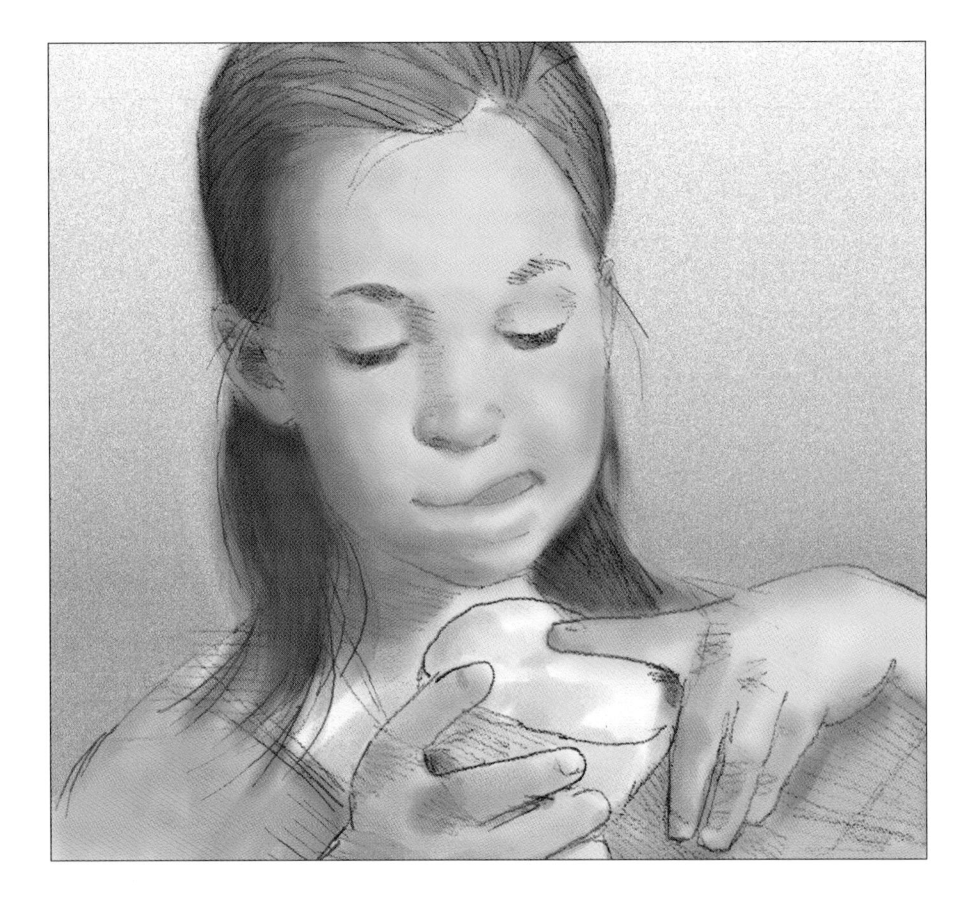

Electra went inside her building, but just before she started up the stairs she took a look at the charlotte russes. Three were much shorter than the others. What would Mama say? Since Electra couldn't make the short ones bigger, the only thing to do was to make the big ones shorter. Electra sat down on the stairs and went to work, smoothing the whipped cream, licking her fingers clean. Finally all the charlotte russes were just about the same height.

Electra started up the stairs again. On the second-floor landing she noticed how lumpy the whipped cream looked. The problem, she decided, came from working with her fingers. She sat down on a step and very delicately ran her tongue around each peak of whipped cream.

They looked better at first, but as Electra climbed up to the third floor they looked more and more uneven. Perhaps it would be best to flatten the whipped cream over the top of each charlotte russe, like icing. Electra sat down and ran the side of her forefinger across the top of each charlotte russe. It took several strokes to get it smooth. The whipped cream was definitely delicious!

Electra climbed up the last flight of stairs. With each step she climbed, the worse she felt. The charlotte russes were a sorry sight with just a thin layer of cream smeared across the top. Electra thought they might look better without any cream at all. So just before she reached the top landing, Electra sat down on the stairs and licked up all the cream from each charlotte russe. They didn't look quite like charlotte russes anymore, but at least they did look all the same.

Electra rang her doorbell and held her breath. What would Mama say?

What Mama said was: "Electra, what happened to the whipped cream on the charlotte russes?"

What Electra said was: "I don't think they're making them with cream anymore."

As soon as she said that, a terrible feeling came over her. She was just about to confess the whole story to Mama when they heard the voices of their guests coming up the stairs.

"Put the box in the kitchen, then go wash your face, brush your hair, and change into your good dress," said Mama. So Electra put the box in the kitchen, and then she washed her face, brushed her hair, and changed into her good dress. She took as long as she could.

When she came out into the parlor, Mrs. Papadapoulos and Mrs. Marcopoulos and Mrs. Marcopoulos's daughter, Athena, and Miss Smith were having tea and dessert. In addition to the charlotte russes there was pastry Mama had made: *baklava* and *diples* and *loukoumades* and *kourabedes*. Electra sat down on the ottoman in front of Mama's chair. Mrs. Papadapoulos was eating one of the former charlotte russes.

"This is very good," she said to Mama. "What's it called?"

Electra looked down at the carpet.

"I don't think it has a name," said Mama. "It's something Electra picked out at the bakery."

Miss Smith said she loved the *baklava*, and asked Mama if she would give her cooking lessons along with her Greek lessons.

Mrs. Marcopoulos asked Mama why Electra wasn't eating any dessert.

"Her tummy isn't feeling too good this afternoon, I'm afraid," said Mama.

"I'm afraid, I'm afraid," said Polo.

"That's a smart bird," said Athena.

"Smart bird!" said Polo, and everyone laughed.

When all the guests had finally gone, Electra asked Mama how she had known about her tummy ache.

"Remorse and too much whipped cream," said Mama, "always cause tummy aches."

"What's remorse?" asked Electra.

"Remorse is when you wish you hadn't done something that you did."

"How did you know about the whipped cream?" asked Electra.

"I know that when you spend a nickel for a charlotte russe, you should always get some whipped cream, too." Mama laughed. "And it was on your face, *Chrisomou,* and in your hair."

"Oh, Mama!" cried Electra, and she climbed on Mama's lap and snuggled into the warmth of her hug.